# Oscar the Button

©Siphano 1997, for the text and illustrations

# 鈕扣奧斯卡
## Oscar the Button

Eszter Nagy 著/繪

張憶萍 譯

三民書局

One day Oscar **popped** out of the coat he was **sewn** and **rolled** away to see the world and find new friends.
Feeling quite pleased and **proud** of his nice **round** shape, he **whistled** as he rolled full-speed towards the village square.

鈕扣奧斯
卡本來是縫
在一件外套上
的，有一天，奧
斯卡從外套上繃
落開來，他要去別
的地方看看這個世
界，順便認識新朋友。
因為對自己圓圓的形狀感
到滿意極了，他便驕傲地吹起
口哨，使盡全力滾向村子裡的廣場。

pop [pɑp] 動 突然地動
sew [so] 動 縫
roll [rol] 動 滾動
proud [praud] 形 驕傲的
round [raund] 形 圓形的
whistle [`hwɪsl̩] 動 吹口哨

He rolled among the houses and up he **climbed** among the roofs.
"Can I play with you?" Oscar asked **politely**.
"Why, you are round!" **replied** the roofs at once. "We are **triangles**. Of course you cannot play with us!"

奧斯卡在一棟一棟的房子之間滾來滾去，然後他爬上屋頂。

「我能跟你們玩嗎？」他很有禮貌地問。

「為什麼？你是圓的！」屋頂馬上回答。「我們是三角形，你當然不能跟我們玩。」

climb [klaɪm] 動 爬
politely [pə`laɪtlɪ] 副 有禮貌地
reply [rɪ`plaɪ] 動 回答
triangle [`traɪˌæŋgl̩] 名 三角形

"What a shame," thought Oscar, a little **discouraged**.
He **set to** rolling again. He rolled on the roadside for hours and hours
without stopping...

「真是可惜。」奧斯卡挫折地想。
他又開始滾動。他沿著馬路不停地賣力滾動
前進，滾了好幾個小時……

discouraged [dɪsˋkɝɪdʒd] 形 洩氣的
set to 開始

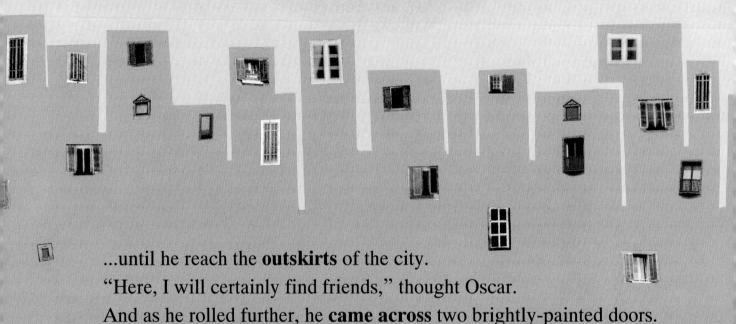

...until he reach the **outskirts** of the city.
"Here, I will certainly find friends," thought Oscar.
And as he rolled further, he **came across** two brightly-painted doors.

……直到他來到了市郊。

「我在這裡一定找得到朋友吧！」奧斯卡心想。

他又繼續前進，直到遇到兩扇漆得很鮮艷的門。

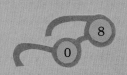

outskirts [ˋaʊtˌskɝts] 名 郊區
come across 偶然遇見

"May I play with you?" he asked them **shyly**.
"**No way!**" replied the doors angrily. "Are you blind or
something? We're **rectangles**, and you're round!"

「我可以跟你們玩嗎？」他害羞地問。
「不要！」這兩扇門很生氣地回答。「你沒看到
嗎？我們是長方形，而你是圓形！」

shyly [ˋʃaɪlɪ] 副 害羞地
No way! 不行
rectangle [ˋrɛkˌtæŋgl̩] 名 長方形

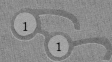

"It's not right," Oscar said to himself.
He was sad and tired, and didn't much **feel like**
rolling any further.
And as he **hesitated** on the edge of the sidewalk,
the wind **blew**...
...and he turned him and **tossed** him and **lifted**
him gently carrying him high into the sky.

「怎麼會這樣呢？」奧斯卡自言自語地說。
他又累又難過，不太想再繼續前進了。
就在他在人行道旁猶豫的時候，一陣風吹了
過來……
風吹動了奧斯卡，並輕輕地將他吹起，把他
高高地帶到空中。

1
2

feel like　想要

hesitate [`hɛzəˌtet] 動 猶豫

blow [blo] 動 吹

toss [tɔs] 動 把…拋起

lift [lɪft] 動 舉起

Oscar saw some **diamonds** from afar...

"Kites," he said to himself and let the wind blow him closer to them.

"Can I join you?" asked Oscar in very little voice.

"This is a **private** club for diamonds, and you, Sir, are round. We **apologize**!" replied the kites, lifting their tails **cautiously**.

奧斯卡看到遠處有一些菱形的東西……

「是風箏。」他對自己說。於是他任由這陣風把自己往風箏吹去。

「我可以加入你們嗎？」奧斯卡用很細小的聲音問。

「這是菱形的私人聚會，而你，先生，是圓形的，所以我們只能對你說抱歉了。」風箏邊回答邊慎重地抬起他們的尾巴。

diamond [`daɪmənd] 名 菱形
private [`praɪvɪt] 形 私人的
apologize [ə`palə,dʒaɪz] 動 道歉
cautiously [`kɔʃəslɪ] 副 小心翼翼地

burst into... 突然…起來

twist [twɪst] 動 盤旋

glide [glaɪd] 動 滑行

glittering [ˈglɪtərɪŋ] 形 閃閃發光的

approach [əˈprotʃ] 動 接近

astonished [əˈstanɪʃt] 形 吃驚的

instant [ˈɪnstənt] 名 立刻

"It's unbearable!" cried Oscar, **bursting into** tears.
And as he shed his tears, he became so light that he
**twisted** and **glided** wherever the wind fancied, rising
higher and higher until, as night was falling, he fell right
into the **glittering** path of the moon.
"Good evening," greeted the moon as Oscar **approached**.
"YOU ARE ROUND!" cried Oscar most **astonished**, and
his tears dried in an **instant**.

「我受不了了！」奧斯卡大叫著哭了起來。
他哭著哭著，發現自己變輕了，他在風裡盤旋、滑翔，然後越飛越高。夜晚來臨時，他正巧落在閃亮的月光下。
「晚安。」當奧斯卡靠近月亮時，月亮向他打了個招呼。
「你是圓的！」奧斯卡吃驚地大叫，眼淚一下子就乾了。

"Of course," replied the moon, "You are not the only one...Round is the earth on which you live, the sun and the **planets**. Cherries and oranges are round, eyes are round, round are the mouths of children when they sing and round are the arms that **embrace**..."

"But shapes are not that important," **continued** the moon. "If you have not yet made friends, it is because you saw only with your eyes...

Tomorrow, you will see better."

「當然，」月亮回答，「你並不孤單……你居住的地球是圓的，太陽和其他的行星也是圓的；櫻桃和柳橙是圓的；眼睛是圓的，小孩子唱歌的嘴巴是圓的；擁抱人的手臂也是圓的……」

「但是形狀並沒有那麼重要，」月亮繼續說，「如果你到現在還沒交到朋友，那是因為你只用眼睛看……明天，你會看得更清楚的。」

planet [`plænɪt] 名 行星
embrace [ɪm`bres] 動 擁抱
continue [kən`tɪnju] 動 繼續（說話）

And so it happened. The next evening the button
returned to earth, and started rolling all over
again. And this time...the world seemed far
more bright and interesting than before.
No sooner did he land...

的ㄉㄜ˙確ㄑㄩㄝˋ。第ㄉㄧˋ二ㄦˋ天ㄊㄧㄢ傍ㄅㄤ˙晚ㄨㄢˇ，奧ㄠˋ斯ㄙ卡ㄎㄚˇ回ㄏㄨㄟˊ到ㄉㄠˋ了ㄌㄜ˙地ㄉㄧˋ面ㄇㄧㄢˋ，又ㄧㄡˋ繼ㄐㄧˋ
續ㄒㄩˋ到ㄉㄠˋ處ㄔㄨˋ滾ㄍㄨㄣˇ動ㄉㄨㄥˋ。而ㄦˊ這ㄓㄜˋ一ㄧˊ次ㄘˋ……世ㄕˋ界ㄐㄧㄝˋ看ㄎㄢˋ起ㄑㄧˇ來ㄌㄞˊ果ㄍㄨㄛˇ然ㄖㄢˊ比ㄅㄧˇ
以ㄧˇ前ㄑㄧㄢˊ明ㄇㄧㄥˊ亮ㄌㄧㄤˋ有ㄧㄡˇ趣ㄑㄩˋ多ㄉㄨㄛ了ㄌㄜ˙。
他ㄊㄚ一ㄧˊ降ㄐㄧㄤˋ落ㄌㄨㄛˋ在ㄗㄞˋ地ㄉㄧˋ上ㄕㄤˋ……

...than he found a job on the **tuxedo** of a **circus magician**.

……就ㄐㄧㄡˋ在ㄗㄞˋ一ㄧ個ㄍㄜˋ馬ㄇㄚˇ戲ㄒㄧˋ團ㄊㄨㄢˊ魔ㄇㄛˊ術ㄕㄨˋ師ㄕ的ㄉㄜ˙小ㄒㄧㄠˇ禮ㄌㄧˇ服ㄈㄨˊ上ㄕㄤˋ找ㄓㄠˇ到ㄉㄠˋ了ㄌㄜ˙
一ㄧ份ㄈㄣˋ工ㄍㄨㄥ作ㄗㄨㄛˋ。

tuxedo [tʌkˋsido] 名 （男子的）小禮服
circus [ˋsɝkəs] 名 馬戲團
magician [məˋdʒɪʃən] 名 魔術師

And all around the magician's top hat he made the most unusual and **amusing** friends. And not all of them were round. But Oscar no longer **bothered** with shapes.

在魔術師的高帽子上，他交到了最特別、最有趣的朋友。雖然不是所有的人都是圓形，但是奧斯卡再也不會為形狀煩惱了。

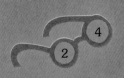

24

amusing [ə`mjuzɪŋ] 形 有趣的
bother [`baðɚ] 動 煩惱

Among all these new friends,
Oscar's best friend **turned out** to be the magician's rabbit.

在所有的新朋友當中，
與奧斯卡最要好的是魔術師的兔子。

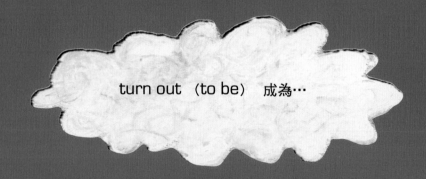

turn out （to be） 成為…

They traveled with the circus around the world
and they always had a great time together.

他們隨著馬戲團到世界各地旅行，
過得非常快樂呢！

## 李恩妙扮裝

Alan MacDonald著／Sally-Anne Lambert繪／楊婗華譯／25開／平裝／56頁／附ＣＤ／定價140元

你參加過化裝遊行嗎？
如果有機會參加，
你最想扮成誰呢？
趕快來看《李恩妙扮裝》，
或許會給你一點靈感喔！

## 李恩剪髮記

Alan MacDonald著／Sally-Anne Lambert繪／張憶萍譯／25開／平裝／56頁／附ＣＤ／定價140元

你怕不怕剪頭髮呢？
當剪髮器在耳邊嗡嗡作響，
你會不會緊張得不敢睜開眼睛？
趕快來看《李恩剪髮記》，
下次你就不會再害怕了喲！

## 莫利伯當家

Sally Grindley著／Tania Hurt-Newton繪／張憶萍譯／25開／平裝／64頁／附ＣＤ／定價140元

你有養寵物嗎？
是小狗、小貓，還是小兔子呢？
不論你的寵物是什麼，
莫利伯都要提醒你，
不要常常把它們獨自留在家裡喲！

## 莫利伯曉家記

Sally Grindley著／Tania Hurt-Newton繪／張憶萍譯／25開／平裝／64頁／附ＣＤ／定價140元

狗狗天生就有冒險犯難的精神，
可是它們還是喜歡溫暖的家，
所以不要忘記把大門關好，
以免它們不小心溜出去，
會找不到回家的路喔！

國家圖書館出版品預行編目資料

鈕扣奧斯卡 / Eszter Nagy著 / 繪；張憶萍
　　譯. －－初版一刷. －－臺北市：三民，
　　民90
　　　　面；　　公分－－（探索英文叢書）
　　中英對照
　　譯自：Oscar le bouton
　　ISBN 957－14－3341－1 （精裝）

　　1.英國語言－讀本

805.18　　　　　　　　　　　　89018050

網路書店位址　http://www.sanmin.com.tw

ⓒ　　鈕扣奧斯卡

著作兼
繪圖者　　Eszter Nagy
譯　者　　張憶萍
發行人　　劉振強
著作財
產權人　　三民書局股份有限公司
　　　　　臺北市復興北路三八六號
發行所　　三民書局股份有限公司
　　　　　地　址／臺北市復興北路三八六號
　　　　　電　話／二五○○六六○○
　　　　　郵　撥／○○○九九九八――五號
印刷所　　臺北市復興北路三八六號
門市部　　復北店／臺北市復興北路三八六號
　　　　　重南店／臺北市重慶南路一段六十一號
初版一刷　中華民國九十年一月
編　號　　S 85509
定　價　　新臺幣壹佰玖拾元整
行政院新聞局登記證局版臺業字第○二○○號

有著作權·不准侵害

ISBN　957－14－3341－1 （精裝）